A Sesame Street Toddler Book

Be My Friend

P9-EIG-764

By Anna Ross • Illustrated by Norman Gorbaty

Random House / Children's Television Workshop

Library of Congress Cataloging-in-Publication Data
Ross, Anna. Be my friend. (A Sesame Street toddler book) Summary: Sesame Street characters demonstrate the positive aspects of having a friend.
[1. Friendship–Fiction.   2. Puppets–Fiction]   I. Gorbaty, Norman, ill.   II. Title.   III. Series. PZ7.R71962Be   1990   [E]
89-24389   ISBN 0-394-85496-9

Manufactured in Singapore   1 2 3 4 5 6 7 8 9 10

A friend is someone
who comes over on
a rainy day.

Won't you be my friend?

A friend is absolutely
the best thing to have
in the whole world.

and wave hello again.

A friend is there to wave
good-bye...

A friend can even
help you hide things.

slide on things,

ride on things.

throw things,

grow things,

taste things,

paste things...

A friend can help you fix things,

mix things,

or a little something to make your doll
feel all better.

A friend knows when you need a
little cheering up...

dress up with,

mess up with.

A friend is
someone to
sing with,

swing with,

and when you don't.

A friend understands when you
want to be alone...

A friend is someone
who doesn't always have
to go first.